JOHN RYAN

Mabel and the Tower of Babel

A LION PICTURE STORY
Oxford · Batavia · Sydney

There was once a king and a queen who ruled over the whole world. They thought they were quite the most important people that had ever been.

But, actually, it wasn't *too* difficult to rule the whole world because at that time everybody spoke the same language.

The king and the queen used to pat one another on the back and tell each other how important they were. They told everybody else, too, and, because it is often the safest thing to do with kings and queens, everybody agreed with them.

The only person who didn't agree with them was their small daughter, Mabel.

Mabel was almost always right.

She said, "Actually, Mama and Papa, you *can't* be the most important people because the most important of all has to be God."

"Rubbish!" said the queen. "*Who* is this God of yours?"

"God made the world and everyone in it," answered Mabel.

7

"Stuff and nonsense!" spluttered the king. "You may think you're right, Mabel, but you're wrong this time. *Where* is this God of yours?"

"Everywhere," answered Mabel. "And up there especially, I think," she added, pointing to the clear blue sky.

"We'll soon see about that," said the king.

"We will indeed!" said the queen. "Only, how?"

"We'll build a tower, the biggest and tallest tower ever made," replied the king. "A tower so high that it will reach all the way to God – if there is such a person. *Then* we'll see who is the most important!" "It won't work," said Mabel, who was almost always right.

So the king sent for his chief builders and told them about the tower. It was to be the biggest and tallest building ever made. Together they worked out how to build it.

Next day, they started work.
Thousands of trees were chopped down. . .

Huge quantities of bricks were baked.
Everything was brought to the spot chosen by
the king.

Just about everybody who was fit to work was
made to help.

Slowly the enormous tower began to rise from the ground.

Every day it got bigger

and taller...

and bigger and taller and taller...

And every day Mabel came out
and looked at it and said,

"It won't work, you know!"

At last the great tower was finished.

"Now," said the king to the queen. "Let us climb to the top with all the people."

"When we get there, first we will declare the tower open. Then we'll see if there's any sign of this God that Mabel is always talking about!"

"I think you're going to be sorry about this," said Mabel.

So the king and the queen climbed all the way to the top of the enormous tower. It was a hot day and they were both red in the face when they got there.

All their subjects went up too. Everybody wanted to see their king open the tower and talk to God.

Just then God looked down from heaven and noticed the tower far below.

"Whatever is that extraordinary little pimple down there?" he asked one of the angels around him. "It looks like an anthill."

"It's a sort of tower, Lord," said an archangel. "The King of the Earth thinks that if he builds high enough, he will be as good as you."

"Shall we knock the tower down, Lord?" asked the archangel. "I have a very handy-sized thunderbolt here."

"No, no," said God. "That would never do. Somebody might get hurt and I'm really very fond of the people on Earth. I have a better idea. I'll make them all speak different languages. Then see what will happen!"

Far down below, at the very tiptop of the tower, the king was beginning his speech.

"Ladies and gentlemen," he announced. "This is a most important – perhaps the most important . . ."

But, even as he was speaking, the strangest thing happened . . .

Hardly anybody could understand a word the king said. Suddenly they were all thinking and speaking different languages of their own.

"Can't hear!" called some.

"Speak up!" cried others.
But most of them shouted, "He's talking poppycock!" – which is not at all the way to address a king.

Moreover, most of the people couldn't understand what their fellows were saying either. There was a great deal of shouting and arguing and waving of hands.

Then everybody started to leave the tower, splitting into groups who found they *could* understand one another.

The king and the queen were left on the top of the tower. They watched their people trailing away into the distance in long straggling lines.

They were all going away to start countries of their own where they could all use the same words and have rulers whom they could understand.

"You see what I mean?" said God to the archangel. "Otherwise the people on Earth will think they can get away with *anything*."

The king and queen made their way down to join the few people who stayed loyal to them.

"It looks to me," said the king, "as though we have a rather small kingdom now. I'm afraid that's the end of being the most important people in the world."

"Told you so!" said Mabel. "You can't beat God!"

And that was the end of the story – except
that they called the tower "Babel", which means a
lot of loud, meaningless words. It also happens to
rhyme with Mabel.

After a while it fell down, because there
weren't enough people around to keep it up.

And Mabel, who was almost always right,
rather wished she hadn't been this time.

It was such hard work trying to learn all the
new different languages!

Text and illustrations copyright © 1990 John Ryan

Published by
Lion Publishing plc
Sandy Lane West, Oxford, England
ISBN 0 7459 2256 2
Albatross Books Pty Ltd
PO Box 320, Sutherland, NSW 2232, Australia
ISBN 0 7324 0561 0

First edition 1990
First paperback edition 1993

A catalogue record for this book is available
from the British Library

Printed and bound in Singapore

Other picture storybooks in paperback from Lion Publishing

Baboushka Arthur Scholey

The Donkey's Day Out Ann Pilling

A Lion for the King Meryl Doney

Papa Panov's Special Day Mig Holder

Stefan's Secret Fear Donna Reid Vann

The Tale of Three Trees Angela Elwell Hunt

The Very Worried Sparrow Meryl Doney